PUFFIN BOOKS

# Space Dog Shock

D1434345

# Space Dog Shock

Written and Illustrated by

## Andrew and Paula Martyr

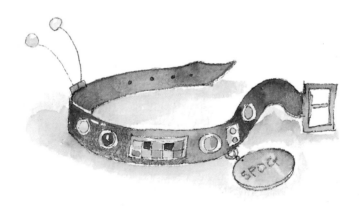

PUFFIN BOOKS

PUFFIN BOOKS
Published by the Penguin Group
Penguin Books Ltd, 80 Strand, London WC2R 0RL, England
Penguin Putnam Inc., 375 Hudson Street, New York, New York 10014, USA
Penguin Books Australia Ltd, Ringwood, Victoria, Australia
Penguin Books Canada Ltd, 10 Alcorn Avenue, Toronto, Ontario, Canada M4V 3B2
Penguin Books India (P) Ltd, 11 Community Centre, Panchsheel Park, New Delhi – 110 017, India
Penguin Books (NZ) Ltd, Cnr Rosedale and Airborne Roads, Albany, Auckland, New Zealand
Penguin Books (South Africa) (Pty) Ltd, 24 Sturdee Avenue, Rosebank 2196, South Africa

Penguin Books Ltd, Registered Offices: 80 Strand, London WC2R 0RL, England

www.penguin.com

First published in Hamish Hamilton Ltd 1997
Published in Puffin Books 1998
5 7 9 10 8 6 4

Text copyright © Andrew Martyr, 1997
Illustrations copyright © Paula Martyr, 1997
All rights reserved

The moral right of the author and illustrator has been asserted

Filmset in Plantin

Printed and bound in China by Leo Paper Products Ltd

British Library Cataloguing in Publication Data
A CIP catalogue record for this book is available from the British Library

ISBN 0–140–38839–7

It all started late one night, long after
Horatio Herbert should have been fast
asleep. Instead he was gazing into the night
from his bedroom window. He was
watching for aliens.

Suddenly he saw something move!
"Perhaps it's an alien," he thought.

But it wasn't.

It was just a dog wearing a strange
collar, sniffing around the rose bushes.

"I expect he's lost," thought Horatio, as
he climbed back into bed, disappointed that
he hadn't seen anything more exciting.

The next morning, the dog was still there, so Horatio decided to investigate. That was when he got his first big shock.

The dog could speak!

"Greetings, small earth person," he said. "I am Spog from outer space, and," he added with a sad sniff, "I am lost."

Horatio couldn't believe his ears.

"Wait till I tell Dad!" he exclaimed.

Horatio found his dad polishing their brand-new car. It was his pride and joy.

"I don't care where the dog comes from," said Mr Herbert sternly, "just keep his muddy feet away from my car."

Horatio's dad obviously didn't believe him.

Neither did Horatio's mum.

"Don't be silly, Horatio," she said. "You don't get dogs in space. There's nowhere to bury bones, for a start!"

"But Mum . . ." Horatio began.

"He can sleep in the old kennel outside," she continued, "and you can take him for a walk . . . when you've tidied up your room."

"Oh no," groaned Horatio, opening his bedroom door. "This will take at least a week."

But Spog shook his head.

Pointing to his collar he said, "I will use my Dogtronic Utility Collar. Just watch this!"

Then Horatio got his second big shock.
Spog quickly pressed some buttons on his
collar and Horatio's old cuddly toy dog
came to life. It had been turned into a
robot!

"Tidy the room, robot," ordered Spog.

Horatio watched, open-mouthed, as the
robot started work.

I am a robot

Soon Horatio's room was tidier than it had ever been. The robot had worked perfectly.

But then the cat walked into the room. The robot pricked up its ears, rolled its eyes, gnashed its teeth and, much to Horatio's horror . . .

. . . WENT QUITE MAD!

It chased the cat three times around the
bedroom . . .

. . . four times up and down the
stairs . . .

. . . and five times in and out of the
kitchen . . .

. . . until finally the robot fell off the
sideboard into Mr Herbert's tropical fish
tank, where it continued to growl and hiss
in a bubbly sort of way.

"A minor fault in the programming, I think," said Spog as the robot settled into a weedy corner of the tank. But Horatio was impressed.

"Can I have a go?" he asked.

"All right," said Spog, handing over the Dogtronic Utility Collar, "but be careful."

Well, it was pure bad luck that Horatio's
mum was just about to use the vacuum
cleaner as Horatio was fiddling about with
the buttons on the Dogtronic Utility Collar.
Suddenly . . .
WHOOSH!

The vacuum cleaner went off like a rocket!

"I think that was the Motor Accelerator button," said Spog, as the vacuum cleaner shot out of the front door with Mrs Herbert clinging on for dear life, and disappeared off along the main road!

It was the police who finally brought Mrs Herbert back home again. She was fined for dangerous driving at 120mph, and the vacuum cleaner was taken away for some scientific tests.

"At least Mum didn't end up in the fish tank," Horatio whispered to Spog.

Horatio's dad was hopping mad.
"There's something very fishy going on
around here!" he thundered.

Horatio was sent up to his bedroom until dinner and Spog was sent out to his kennel.

However, as Horatio sat gloomily on his bed, he couldn't help thinking that there might be more trouble in store.

At last it was time for dinner and Horatio
was allowed downstairs. Mrs Herbert was
just dishing up when Horatio noticed a loud
rumbling noise coming from the garden.

It grew louder and louder, until the whole
house was shaking.

They all rushed outside . . .

. . . just in time to see Spog heading off towards outer space!

This time he had used his Dogtronic Utility Collar to turn his kennel into a spaceship!

Up and up and up it went, until suddenly . . .

DISASTER!

The main engines failed!

Luckily Spog managed to get out and open his parachute just in time as the spaceship started to come back down . . . and down . . . and down . . .

. . . heading straight for Mr Herbert's brand-new car!

CRASH!

Nuts and bolts and springs and screws flew everywhere. The car was smashed to smithereens.

"Oh dear!" said Horatio.

"Oh dear, oh dear!" said his mum.

"Just wait until I get my hands on that dog," growled his dad.

That was when Horatio had his last big
shock.

Suddenly, another spaceship appeared in
the sky – ten times bigger than Spog's had
been.

It came down slowly and landed on the
lawn. The hatch opened with a loud hiss
and out stepped two more spacedogs!

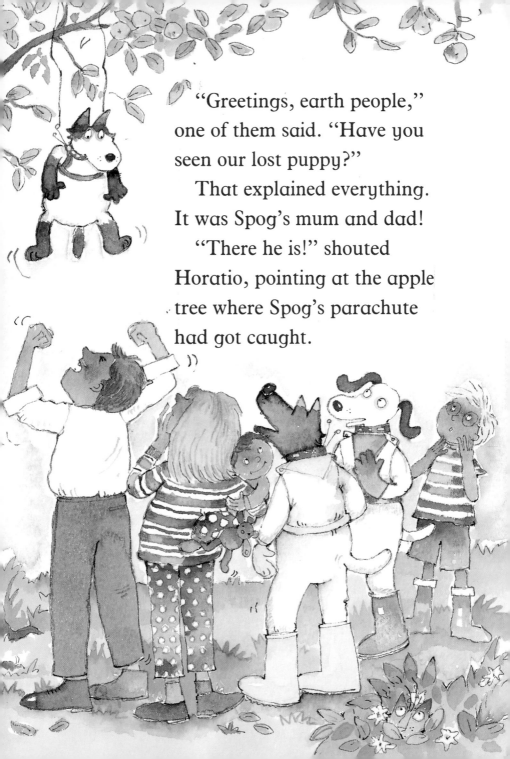

"Greetings, earth people," one of them said. "Have you seen our lost puppy?"

That explained everything. It was Spog's mum and dad!

"There he is!" shouted Horatio, pointing at the apple tree where Spog's parachute had got caught.

Well, as you can imagine, Spog got a
good telling-off from his mum and dad for
running away like that, and for causing so
much trouble.

He had his Dogtronic Utility Collar
confiscated for three whole weeks!

Luckily, Spog's mum and dad had plenty
of robots on their spaceship that didn't
chase cats. They were soon put to work
mending Mr Herbert's car.

Horatio and Spog helped to show them
where all the bits went, too!

The car was soon as good as new. (Well, almost.)

When it was ready they all went for a test drive and, even though it did look a bit odd, it went like a dream.

Horatio's dad couldn't wait to give it a polish!

At last, after a special tea on the
spaceship, it was time for Spog to go home.

Horatio was quite sad really.

"Can he come to stay in the school
holidays?" Horatio asked his mum.

"I suppose so," she sighed, "on one condition – that he doesn't bring his Dogtronic Utility Collar with him!"

Phew!

*Also available in First Young Puffin*

## ERIC'S ELEPHANT ON HOLIDAY
### John Gatehouse

When Eric and his family go on holiday to the seaside, Eric's elephant goes too. Everyone is surprised – and rather cross – to find a big white elephant on the beach. But the elephant soon amazes them with her jumbo tricks and makes it a very special holiday indeed!

## ROLL UP! ROLL UP! IT'S RITA
### Hilda Offen

Rita is furious when she finds everyone has gone to the fair without her. She's going to miss the fancy dress competition and a balloon ride. Then Rita remembers her Rescuer's outfit. Soon she's ready to thrill the crowd with some amazing stunts!

## WOOLLY JUMPERS
### Peta Blackwell

Mabel Cablestitch loves knitting. But when she is given a new pair of knitting needles strange things start to happen. Woolly animals appear as if by magic. What on earth is going on?